Mookey
the Monkey
Gets Over Being Teased

For David — HSL
To Rosie, my own little monkey — MR

Published by
MAGINATION PRESS
An Educational Publishing Foundation Book
American Psychological Association
750 First Street, NE
Washington, DC 20002

For more information about our books, including a complete catalog,
please write to us, call 1-800-374-2721,
or visit our website at www.maginationpress.com.

Editor: Darcie Conner Johnston
Art Director: Susan K. White
Printed by Worzalla, Stevens Point, Wisconsin

Library of Congress Cataloging-in-Publication Data

Lonczak, Heather Suzanne.
Mookey the monkey gets over being teased /
by Heather Lonczak ; illustrated by Marcy Ramsey.
p. cm.
Summary: Teased by his classmates because he is hairless, Mookey the monkey
discovers there are many ways to handle teasing and still remain true to oneself.
ISBN-13: 978-1-59147-479-1 (hardcover : alk. paper)
ISBN-10: 1-59147-479-5 (hardcover : alk. paper)
ISBN-13: 978-1-59147-480-7 (pbk. : alk. paper)
ISBN-10: 1-59147-480-9 (pbk. : alk. paper)
[1. Monkeys—Fiction. 2. Teasing—Fiction. 3. Self-confidence—Fiction.
4. Animals—Fiction. 5. Schools—Fiction.]
I. Ramsey, Marcy Dunn, ill. II. Title.
PZ7.L8418Moo 2006
[E]—dc22   2006009947

10 9 8 7 6 5 4 3 2 1

Mookey
the Monkey
Gets Over Being Teased

by Heather Lonczak

illustrated by Marcy Ramsey

MAGINATION   NGTON, D.C.

Once upon a time in a faraway jungle,
a tiny monkey was born without a single hair on his body.
No fur, no fleece, not even fuzz!
His parents named their beloved baby Mookey.
They found his soft, alabaster skin beautiful.
His aunties and uncles and cousins took turns caressing
his silky head, and his nana knitted cozy sweaters
to keep him warm in the winter.

As Mookey grew, he stayed as hairless as the day he was born.
"I'm as smooth as a banana," he said with pride.
He loved the colorful clothes he wore to keep warm in the
winter and to avoid sunburn in the summer.

On his first day of school, Mookey picked out his favorite jungle outfit. His parents gave him a big book bag. His nana gave him new shoes for his smooth feet. Everyone kissed Mookey's sweet pink cheeks and wished him a great day.

But things didn't work out so well.

Mookey's classmates had never seen a hairless monkey.

They didn't know what to think. Some were not very nice.

On Monday, Morton Mongoose called him Baldy.

On Tuesday, Tristan Tiger just stared.

On Wednesday, Wilhelmina Warthog pointed and giggled.

Every day they teased Mookey. And soon he stopped loving the very thing he once loved most about himself.

"Why do I have to be different?" he thought. "It's not fair." Then he had an idea.

At Crocodile Clyde's Costume Shop,
Mookey found what he was looking for.

The next morning he arrived at school as furry as everyone else.
But soon it didn't seem like such a good idea.
"This is hotter than a polar bear coat!"

Gluing fur clippings from
Beatrice Baboon's Beauty Boutique
didn't work either.

At Paulina Porcupine's Potions, Mookey bought a bottle of Potion No. 114, which Paulina said would help grow hair. The next morning he rubbed it on his skin. Soon his skin started to tingle. "Something is growing!" he rejoiced.

But it wasn't hair.

"Nothing works," grumbled Mookey.

"Who, whooo,
I've been watching you,
Mookey," said Oslo Owl.
"You can't solve your problems
by changing who you are on the outside.
And you can't change others.
But you *can* change what you do when someone teases you."
"How?" asked Mookey.
"You are surrounded by wisdom and experience,"
Oslo hooted, but said nothing more.

"What does he mean?" Mookey asked Horatio Hyena.
"I think he means your friends can help," said Horatio.
So Mookey told Horatio about his problem.
"When folks give me the business," said Horatio,
"I just make a joke!
It's hard for others to laugh at you
when you're already laughing."

"Is that so?" said Mookey.
"I know some funny jokes. And I like to laugh!"
Mookey thanked Horatio and went on his way.

"Hellooooo," Mookey called up to Genevieve Giraffe.

"May I ask your advice?"

Genevieve listened to Mookey's story.

"When I was your age," she said, "kids called me Stretch.

But one summer there was a drought, and the only food was too

high in the trees for anyone to reach. Anyone except me, that is.

So I shook down all the bananas and coconuts."

"Then I felt good about my long neck,
and when I did, so did everyone else.
That helped me ignore kids when they teased me."
"Hmmm," thought Mookey out loud.
"My sleek skin helps me swim fast. I feel good about that."
"That could surely come in handy some day," she said.
Mookey thanked her and
went on his way.

Sigmund Sloth dangled sleepily overhead.

"What's up?" he yawned.

Mookey told him his story.

"I have especially long toes," said Sigmund.

"Sometimes Winky Wolfhound gives me a hard time about it.

But I just take a deep breath and relax, and go back to my nap.

He always finds that boring, so he leaves me alone.

Apparently teasing Howie Howler-Monkey is more fun."

"Hmmm," said Mookey,
"I do get upset when they tease me.
I'll try breathing and walking away instead."
Mookey turned to thank Sigmund,
but he was already asleep.

Mookey caught up with Giselle Gazelle, the mail carrier. "There have always been creatures in this village who are unkind to gazelles. I've accepted that," she said after hearing Mookey's story.

"I spend time with Zoe Zebra and Abraham Antelope.
They are nice. I try to avoid the others."
"Hmmm, Otis Orangutan has always been friendly," said Mookey.
But he said it to the air.
Giselle was already well on her way!

Mookey swung home to his parents.

"It's not easy being teased," he told them.

"But everyone I talked to had a good idea."

"We're so sorry for what you've been going through," said his mom.

"But we're very proud of you for asking for help," said his pop.

"Why do kids tease each other?"
Mookey wanted to know.
"Maybe so they can feel better about themselves,"
said his mom.
"Maybe because they feel uncomfortable
when someone is different," said his pop.
"It's not about you," they said.
"It's more about them."

Back at school, Mookey had lots of new tools to help him
deal with being teased. He felt like he was wearing a suit of armor
over his smooth skin, just like Arty Armadillo!

Over time, Mookey tried all of his friends' ideas.

Some kids became bored.

Some thought Mookey was funny.

And some saw him in a brand new light.

Of course, Mookey still got teased
from time to time.
But it didn't bother him like it used to.

Sometimes he even took it
as a compliment.
"That's right," he would say proudly,
"I *am* a hairless monkey.
Thank you for noticing!"

NOTE TO PARENTS AND TEACHERS
by Jane Annunziata, Psy.D.

Teasing is one of the facts of life of childhood. From occasional poking fun by an older sibling, to very hurtful comments made frequently and over a long span of time by a number of kids, the range of experience is broad. Fortunately, most childhood teasing is more benign, and it resolves fairly quickly when children are given helpful suggestions for coping with it.

That said, teasing can be very upsetting to a child, even when it doesn't seem serious from an adult perspective. Sometimes adults minimize the effect of teasing because it is so common, or they don't realize how bad it makes the child feel. Even children themselves can minimize the effects and either don't tell their parents or teachers, or they put on a happy face that hides their underlying pain.

Whether they show it or not, when children are teased they usually feel an array of emotions that may include confusion, anger, self-blame, sadness, embarrassment, and loss of control. How much they suffer depends on the amount of teasing they receive, how hurtful it is, how much it taps an existing issue (such as weight, height, or learning disability), how parents and teachers handle it, how resilient the child is, and most importantly, how well armed the child is with effective ways to cope.

Adults are most helpful when they take teasing seriously—without going too far and overreacting, as this will intensify the child's own concerns. It is particularly important that parents and teachers respond when the child seems upset or when the teasing taps an existing concern. When children are already sensitive to things about themselves, even somewhat good-natured teasing can feel hurtful.

The importance of empowering children by teaching them coping techniques cannot be overstated. Knowing how to respond to teasing helps children in two ways: They can keep the teasing in perspective, and they feel armed to face the teasers. Ultimately, these skills give children the ability to put garden-variety teasing in the category of just another hurdle of childhood.

COPING TECHNIQUES FOR CHILDREN
Mookey the Monkey Gets Over Being Teased illustrates many helpful strategies for children to learn and use:

Be yourself. Trying to be like everyone else doesn't work, but standing out or trying to be purposely different doesn't help diminish teasing—and can exacerbate it.

Think positive. Think of differences as desirable strengths, and keep in mind that the focus of today's teasing may well become a future asset. A tall girl will someday embrace and enjoy her height. A very bright child who is teased for being "brainy" may someday be very successful.

Stick with friends. Build a circle of peers who are friendly and nice, and let these friends know their support is needed when teasing is a problem.

Ask for help. Ask others who are trustworthy (peers and adults) for help about coping with teasing, especially if it's getting worse. Express feelings about being teased to a supportive adult or a good friend.

Use humor. A sense of humor about oneself especially disarms the teaser and tends to diminish the teasing.

Ignore the teasing. Don't pay attention to the teasing, act as though it is not bothersome or upsetting, or simply walk away. Plenty of research shows that ignoring an undesirable behavior tends to extinguish that behavior. This applies to teasing too.

Stay cool. Use techniques to stay calm and relaxed rather than responding in an upset manner, which increases the teasing. Taking deep breaths and visualizing a favorite place or a happy image are simple yet effective relaxation techniques.

Teasing happens. It's helpful to accept the fact that there will always be teasing and teasers. Kids can't control that, but they can control how they react. There are many ways to react that make a kid feel better about himself and diminish the teasing.

It's not about you. Understand that teasing has to do with the *teaser*, not with the child who is being teased. Believing that it's the teaser who has a problem really helps children cope and hold on to their self-esteem.

In addition to Mookey's techniques outlined above, here are a few other strategies that adults can help children use:

Read and re-read books like *Mookey*. This will refresh the child's skill set and help him remember that the teasing will lessen and eventually stop. Also, use the book to help the child brainstorm about other things Mookey could say or do, and help the child transfer those solutions from Mookey's situation to his own.

Take control. Help the child take control of the teasing when and where she can. Without implying that the teasing is her fault, help her think of things she can change to lessen the teasing. It can be empowering for her to take control. This might be as simple as walking to school on the opposite side of the street from the teaser, or wearing more age-appropriate clothes.

Strong presence. Brainstorm with the child about ways he can feel stronger and less vulnerable to teasing. Helping him feel stronger inside (by arming him with coping techniques), and helping him feel physically stronger (e.g., through exercise) can help him develop a stronger presence to himself and to others.

Other helpers. Suggest that the child talk to a school guidance counselor or other adult she views as helpful (such as a tutor or coach) for ideas and strategies. Sometimes an older child or sibling can be a good resource too. They may well give the same advice that a parent or teacher does, but the child may absorb it in a different way if it comes from a different source. (Make sure these individuals have good judgment and will give the child good advice!)

WHAT PARENTS CAN DO

Get the teasing on the table if you know it is happening and your child isn't raising it with you. Some children feel too hurt or embarrassed about the teasing to raise it with their parents. Talking about it directly begins the problem-solving process.

Notify your child's teachers so that they can be on the lookout for the teasing, involve the school guidance counselor if necessary, and offer your child extra support as needed.

Find peer environments where there is greater acceptance and tolerance of all children (e.g., Scouts, church groups). This not only provides another arena for feeling validated by peers, but also helps to counteract the negative effects of teasing in the classroom.

Make sure that you are aware of any teasing within your own family, and don't allow any that seems hurtful or excessive. Many parents are too accepting of the teasing that occurs within the family (especially by older siblings) and minimize its negative impact. Teasing at home is especially problematic when the child is already being teased at school.

Help your child express the array of feelings she has about being teased. While placing the emphasis on coping techniques, give her plenty of room to talk about and "have" her feelings about being teased. Offer alternatives to talking about feelings, such as self-expression through drawing or journaling, or exercising to release feelings.

Speaking to the teasing comments is helpful and gives perspective. For example, if your child is being teased about being short, you can say, "We have a lot of height in our family, and you will grow taller soon."

Lend your child your optimism and future view that the teasing will stop and he will feel better. It is easy for children to lose perspective and future hope when they are upset. Remind your child that although he feels upset now, it won't always be this way, and the tools he has will work. Life will get better.

WHAT TEACHERS CAN DO

Be on the lookout. A teased child doesn't always come forward to talk about it, and those who tease often do it when adults are not supervising closely, such as during recess or while walking to school.

Notify parents that the child is being teased at school. Schedule a parent-teacher meeting so that everyone can brainstorm together about ways to help the child both at school and at home.

Notify the guidance counselor of the problem. The counselor can then meet individually with the child who is being teased, when that would be helpful. In more serious cases, the counselor can also work with the teasers to stop the problem. It is important to let children know that their school will not tolerate hurtful or excessive teasing.

Do a general unit in the classroom on being a good friend and the importance of being respectful and kind to one another.

Offer the child suggestions for coping with the teasing. These may not be any different from those offered by the parents, but sometimes children hear it better when it comes from someone else.

Notify the parents if the child is suffering from the teasing and may benefit from professional help.

WHEN CHILDREN NEED MORE HELP

Fortunately, most teasing is short-lived and benign. Parents and teachers (who survived it themselves) can help children get through it by teaching them empowering coping skills and normalizing the experience of childhood teasing. Teasing is obviously more concerning when it escalates, is frequent, happens with several children rather than one or two teasers, and is occurring in more than one place (e.g., school, sports team, the neighborhood, etc.).

When teasing is more pervasive and the child is visibly upset by it, consultation with a mental health professional may be indicated. A therapist who specializes in work with children and families will not only help the child with the upset feelings but will also work with parents so that they can support their child through this stress. Answering yes to any of the questions below suggests that professional assistance may be needed.

❖ Does the teasing overlap with an existing issue or area of sensitivity for the child?

❖ Has the teasing gone on for more than three weeks?

❖ Does the child want to avoid places where the teasing occurs? For example, does she want to skip softball practice because she is being teased there?

❖ Does the child seem quite bothered by the teasing? In other words, does the child seem anxious about it, talk frequently about it, or cry when discussing it?

❖ Have you noticed changes in your child's mood or behavior? For example, does your child seem sad, anxious, quiet, or withdrawn? Has the child begun to misbehave at home or school?

Remember, all children experience some amount of teasing during their young lives. The key is to provide them with assistance (at home and school or with a professional if needed) so that this obstacle of childhood can be overcome.

Jane Annunziata, Psy.D., is a clinical psychologist with a private practice for children and families in McLean, Virginia. She is also the author of many books and articles addressing the concerns of children and their parents.

ABOUT THE AUTHOR

HEATHER LONCZAK, Ph.D., is an educational psychologist with expertise in at-risk youth and positive youth development. She has published a number of scholarly articles focusing on adolescent well-being, and this is her second work of fiction for children. She lives in Seattle with her husband and two children.

ABOUT THE ILLUSTRATOR

The daughter of an artist, MARCY RAMSEY grew up with drawing pencils and paintbrushes in her hands, and has illustrated more than 50 books and written stories of her own. She lives on the Chesapeake Bay in Maryland.